P9-BZX-286

For Henry

I Am a Witch's Cat. Copyright © 2014 by Harriet Muncaster. All rights reserved.
Manufactured in China.
No part of this book may be used or reproduced in any manner whatsoever without written permission
except in the case of brief quotations embodied in critical articles and reviews.
For information address HarperCollins Children's Books, a division of HarperCollins Publishers,
10 East 53rd Street, New York, NY 10022. www.harpercollinschildrens.com

Library of Congress Cataloging-in-Publication Data
Muncaster, Harriet.
I am a witch's cat / by Harriet Muncaster. — 1st ed.
        p.   cm.
    Summary: A "special witch's cat" is certain her mother is a witch because she keeps special
potions in the bathroom, grows magical herbs in her garden, and whirls her broomstick around the
room once a week.
    ISBN 978-0-06-222914-4 (hardcover bdg.)
    [1. Witches—Fiction.   2. Cats—Fiction.]   I. Title.
PZ7.M92325Iaf   2014   2012022152
[E]—dc23   CIP
                                                                                        AC

The artist used fabric, watercolor, pen and ink, and a variety of media to create flat images and three-
dimensional scenes, which were photographed and digitized to create the illustrations for this book.
Star patterned fabric design by Elizabeth Miles
Design and typography by Martha Rago. Hand lettering by Stephen Rapp
14 15 16 17 18 SCP 10 9 8 7 6 5 4 3 2 1
❖
First Edition

FREDERICK COUNTY PUBLIC LIBRARIES

I AM A WITCH'S CAT

Harriet Muncaster

HARPER
An Imprint of HarperCollinsPublishers

My mom is a witch,
and I am her special witch's cat.

I know my mom is a witch because she keeps lots
of strange potion bottles in the bathroom that
I am NOT allowed to touch.

And when we go shopping, she buys

jars of EYEBALLS and GREEN FINGERS.

But I don't mind, because she is a good witch.

I know my mom is a witch

because she grows magical herbs in the garden . . .

. . . and then uses them to make
bubbling, hissing potions. Sometimes she lets me stir.
Being a witch's cat is a VERY important job.

I know my mom is a witch because when her friends come over, they sit in a circle and CACKLE and swap spell books. They pat my head and say, "My, how you've grown!" And I PURR to show them how much I love being a witch's cat.

I know my mom is a witch because whenever
I hurt myself, she MAGICS it all better.
Sometimes witches' cats have to be very brave.

I know my mom is a witch because once a week she gets out her broomstick and whirls it around my room. Sometimes she lets me have a ride. That is the BEST thing about being a witch's cat.

On Friday nights my mom goes out and
the babysitter comes. I don't mind,
because the babysitter is nice.

She lets me watch TV and eat popcorn
until it is time to go to bed.

I don't know where my mom goes. She's always
my mom, but I think that sometimes she just
needs a break from being a witch.

AUG 2014

2 1982 02835 2460